Briggsy's Time to Shine

Linda McKinley

Illustrated by Dwight Nacaytuna.

To order additional copies of this book, contact:
Xlibris
1-888-795-4274
www.Xlibris.com
Orders@Xlibris.com

ISBN: Softcover   978-1-7960-7659-2
       EBook   978-1-7960-7658-5

Print information available on the last page

Rev. date: 12/05/2019

For

Patrick

My favorite *little* music maker

With love

Acknowledgments

Thank you to the publishing staff I have been in contact with, for their help and guidance. Thanks also to my family and friends, big and small, who have taken the time to read this little book, and to Chris McKinley for the back cover photo. Finally, a big shout out to all the little "Briggsys" everywhere, who hopefully will get their time to shine!

The children in Miss Poppy's kindergarten music class were very excited on their first day of school. It was a chilly autumn morning, and Miss Poppy had just told them that they could each choose a musical instrument they would like to play. "Children, we will have so much fun this year learning to play the instruments you select, and if we practice every day, we can have our very own band."

"Yippee!" shouted the children. They all loved the idea of being in a band! "Come with me," Miss Poppy said, and the children followed their teacher to the back of the classroom.

Little instruments, specially made for little hands, were spread out on a big table. There was a clarinet named Toodle-Oo Pete, whose music sounded just like his name. He looked like a big licorice stick. In fact, Miss Poppy said clarinets were sometimes called licorice sticks. "That's because they look like a real stick, and they're black, like licorice candy," she said.

Pete looked a bit puzzled when he heard Miss Poppy say that. "I sure hope nobody takes a bite out of me," he said, in his toodle-oo voice, and everyone laughed.

"Hey kids, over here," squawked Bo, the saxophone. "I'm just like candy too. That's because I play really sweet music." he said, laughing at his own joke. Another funny thing about Bo was, if you didn't play him the right way, he sometimes made strange honking noises, like a goose. Just then he honked to prove it. "Honk honk"! and the children squealed with delight!

"Excusez-moi, excuse me! What about *moi*?" chimed in Louis, the French horn. Even though he was shaped like a twisty pretzel, his music was soft and mellow, and easy on the ears. "It takes a big breath of air to get a sound out of me, but in the end, it's worth it," boasted Louis. All the children made ooh, and ahh sounds, and were very impressed with Louis' smooth velvety tones.

"Hey you guys, don't forget it takes a lot of air for me as well," tooted Ty, the trumpet. He was sometimes called a horn, and was quite handsome, all brassy and shiny.

"Ty is a good solo instrument," Miss Poppy said, proudly. "Solo means, he sounds just fine all by himself."

"Thank you very much," mumbled Ty. He seemed a little embarrassed. "I'm not one to toot my own horn. All you have to do is blow into my mouthpiece, and presto, out comes a 'rooty tooty' sound." The children thought that was so funny. "And I must admit, my high notes are my best feature," he bragged.

"Ty may play high notes, but not as high as I can," trilled Lilly, the piccolo. She was proud that she had the highest voice of all the instruments. She thought she sounded just like a songbird, and delighted the children by warbling a few notes. They all giggled, and agreed Lilly really did sound like a bird.

Finally there were two percussion instruments. "Percussion means these instruments have to be struck, or hit, to make music," explained Miss Poppy.

"It doesn't hurt though" boomed Buddy, the drum. He liked it when his drumsticks made a rat-a-tat sound to set the beat, or the rhythm of the music. "Miss Poppy's piano is a percussion instrument too," said Miss Poppy. The piano was Miss Poppy's instrument, and she played it every day when the children sang songs or moved to the music.

Winnie, the xylophone, was Buddy's best percussion pal. "Winnie needs special sticks, called mallets, to run up and down her keys," said Miss Poppy. "They make 'ding dong' sounds, like a doorbell ringing. The long keys make low sounds, and the short keys make high pitched sounds. Winnie is lucky because she can be played standing up, sitting on a table, or on someone's lap," said Miss Poppy. The children thought, wow! Winnie was very talented to be able to do all three.

Miss Poppy still hadn't noticed Briggsy, the tuba, who was hiding. He had managed to scoot off the big table and was now sitting on the floor. He was under a nearby table because the other instruments teased him, and often said mean things like, "hey Briggsy, you need a tune-up," or "you're too big, and way too loud." Sadly, their unkind words hurt Briggsy's feelings. He was tired of being bullied.

He still enjoyed Miss Poppy's music class though, even if there were times he wished he was home with Mama and Papa Tuba.

Finally all the instruments had been chosen except Briggsy. He suddenly discovered how disappointed he was. "I always wanted to be in a band. I should never have hidden under this table," he said quietly, talking to himself. He tried to be brave and not cry, even though he felt like it. "Maybe I am too big and too loud, like they said. Mama Tuba always told me I was just big for my age. And it would be so nice if I could play more than *oom pah pahs*." I even hurt my own ears sometimes Briggsy thought. He was starting to feel more and more sorry for himself.

"Don't worry, Briggsy," boomed Buddy the drum, who happened to overhear what Briggsy said. "That's how you and I are supposed to sound. We are who we are." Briggsy thought for a moment about what Buddy said, and then replied, "But I don't like who I am," and as hard as he tried, he couldn't stop the tears from rolling down his cheeks.

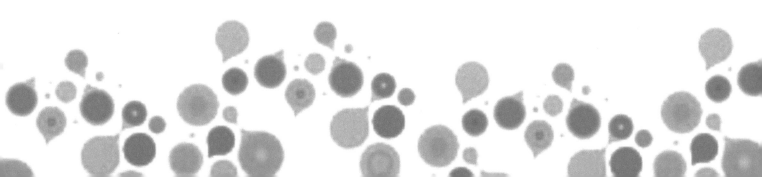

But then he thought about Mama Tuba tucking him in his tuba case at night, and saying, "Briggsy, so what if you're big and a bit loud. It's more important to be proud of who you are on the inside. Don't forget, you're named after a famous tuba player, Pete Briggs. He played happy music on an instrument just like you. Your time to shine will come."

Suddenly, thinking about Mama Tuba's words made Briggsy feel very important. After all, he was named after a big tuba star!

A few weeks later, Miss Poppy's "K" band was practicing a new song in music class, when a little boy named Paulo came into the classroom. He seemed frightened and a bit shy because he didn't know anyone. Miss Poppy greeted him with a warm smile. "Children, come and meet our new friend, Paulo. Please use your very best manners, and make him feel welcome."

The children seemed excited that they were going to have a new student in class, and gathered around Paulo. They shook his hand, saying, "Good morning Paulo. We're happy to meet you. We have lots of fun in music class, and we hope you like it too." Paulo was feeling better already.

Just then, in a far corner of the room, Paulo noticed something. *I must be seeing things*, he thought. He ran over to investigate. "Oh *Chico*, oh boy! It's *mi instrumento favorito!*" The other instruments were very surprised. Could he be talking about Briggsy? "*Amo la tuba*! I love the tuba!" said Paulo. "I played it at my other school. My teacher said I played *bueno*. May I play it now, *por favor*?"

When Briggsy heard that, he couldn't believe his ears. His cheeks puffed out when Paulo picked him up, and they began making such happy music, that all the children began clapping their hands and dancing. Miss Poppy started dancing too. Even the other instruments seemed happy for Briggsy. They were flabbergasted that he was making such happy peppy music!

Pete, the clarinet called out, "Hey, guys! Get a load of Briggsy! He's got a good sound after all! He's really something!" It was then that the other instruments began to realize how unkind they had been, and felt sorry they had teased Briggsy so much. They had thought it was all in fun, and didn't realize it had made Briggsy feel sad.

"Hey, "Briggs," they shouted, "welcome to the band! You're the best! And just like that, something wonderful was happening in Miss Poppy's music class. All the instruments started cheering and shouting, "Hooray for Briggsy! hooray for Briggsy!"

Briggsy felt so proud he thought he was going to bust. *Mama Tuba was right*, he thought. *She said my time to shine would come. I now have a new friend, and the other instruments think I'm cool!*

Briggsy wanted the whole world to know how happy he was. He puffed out his cheeks even more, took a deep breath, and blew an extra big *oom pah pah.* And this time, it was *super duper LOUD*!

CPSIA information can be obtained
at www.ICGtesting.com
Printed in the USA
LVHW071126221219
641383LV00017B/1910/P